What has 4 wheels and flies?

A garbage truck.

How do you make the number one disappear?

Add a "g" and it's gone.

Where does 9 plus 4 equal 1?

On a clock.

Nice belt.

If 10 bugs bug 2 rhinos, what time is it?

10 cats are in a boat and 1 jumps out. How many are left?

10 after 2.

None because they were copycats.

For Edie St. John McMillan, friends since Bluebirds —J.S.

For Renita Brown, who always saw the best in everyone. We will miss her. —M.B.

NOTICE

THIS IS A BORZOI BOOK PUBLISHED BY ALFRED A. KNOPF

Text copyright © 2019 by Judy Sierra
Jacket art and interior illustrations copyright © 2019 by Marc Brown

All rights reserved. Published in the United States by Alfred A. Knopf, an imprint of
Random House Children's Books, a division of Penguin Random House LLC, New York.

Knopf, Borzoi Books, and the colophon are registered trademarks of Penguin Random House LLC.

Visit us on the Web! rhcbooks.com

Educators and librarians, for a variety of teaching tools, visit us at
RHTeachersLibrarians.com

Library of Congress Cataloging-in-Publication Data is available upon request.
ISBN 978-0-525-64620-4 (trade) — ISBN 978-0-525-64621-1 (lib. bdg.) — ISBN 978-0-525-64622-8 (ebook)

The text of this book is set in 24-point Kosmik.
The illustrations were created using gouache and pencil.

MANUFACTURED IN CHINA
September 2019
10 9 8 7 6 5 4 3 2 1

First Edition

EveryOne COUNts

by Judy Sierra

illustrated by

Marc Brown

ALFRED A. KNOPF

New York

It started out small, with no creatures at all,
Just a musty old, dusty old tumbledown mall.
Then along came Takoda the tiger cub, who
Saw the tumbledown mall and imagined a zoo.
But to build a new zoo takes a mighty big crew.

Two rough, tough rhinos arrived with a crash.
And they swept out the mall, and they bulldozed the trash.

A cricket jumped up,   then an ant,   then a bee.

A rhinoceros beetle,   a wasp,   and a flea.

A spider,   a mantis,   a moth,

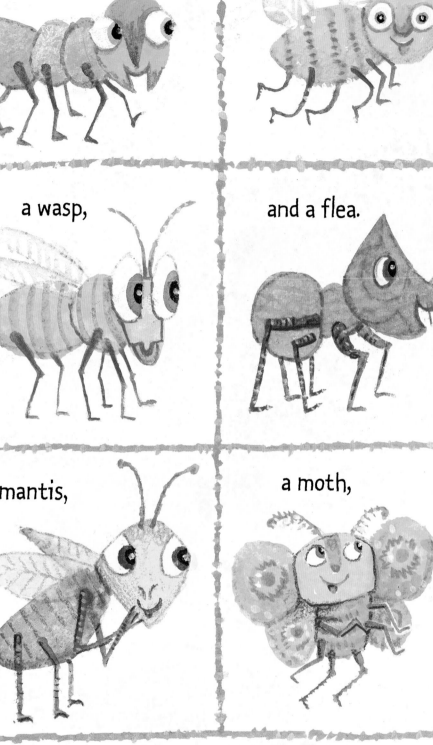

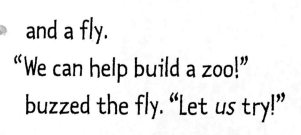

and a fly.
"We can help build a zoo!"
buzzed the fly. "Let *us* try!"

"Not a chance," said the rhinos.
"You bugs are too small."
"You're pests. You're annoying.
 You don't count at all."

3 Three lemurs rolled paint on the walls and the stairs.

Four oryx cut windows (some circles, some squares).

Five bears carved out burrows, and tunnels, and lairs.

LIONS'
LAIR

Six giraffes raised up towers much taller than trees.

Seven bats lifted banners that blew in the breeze.

9 Nine moose dug a moat (nine feet deep, nine feet wide).

10 Ten crocodiles sculpted a grand waterslide.
They asked all of their friends to climb up for a ride.

But two rough, tough rhinos were blocking the way,
Snorting, "This is *our* slide. No one else gets to play."

Then silently, stealthily, down from the sky
Came the spider, the mantis, the moth, and the fly.
Along with the cricket, the ant, and the bee.
The rhinoceros beetle, the wasp, and the flea.

One bug crept in each ear, while three snuck up each snout.
Do bugs really count? We're about to find out.

10-9-8-7-6-5-4-3-2-1

Two rough, tough rhinos sneezed—

ah-ah-ah-CHOO!

As into the air they flipped and they flew.

ah-ah-ah-

The rhinos were rubbing their noses and ears,
Crying nearly one thousand rhinoceros tears.
"We're sorry," they blubbered, "for bullying you.
We're rough and we're tough, but we don't rule the zoo."

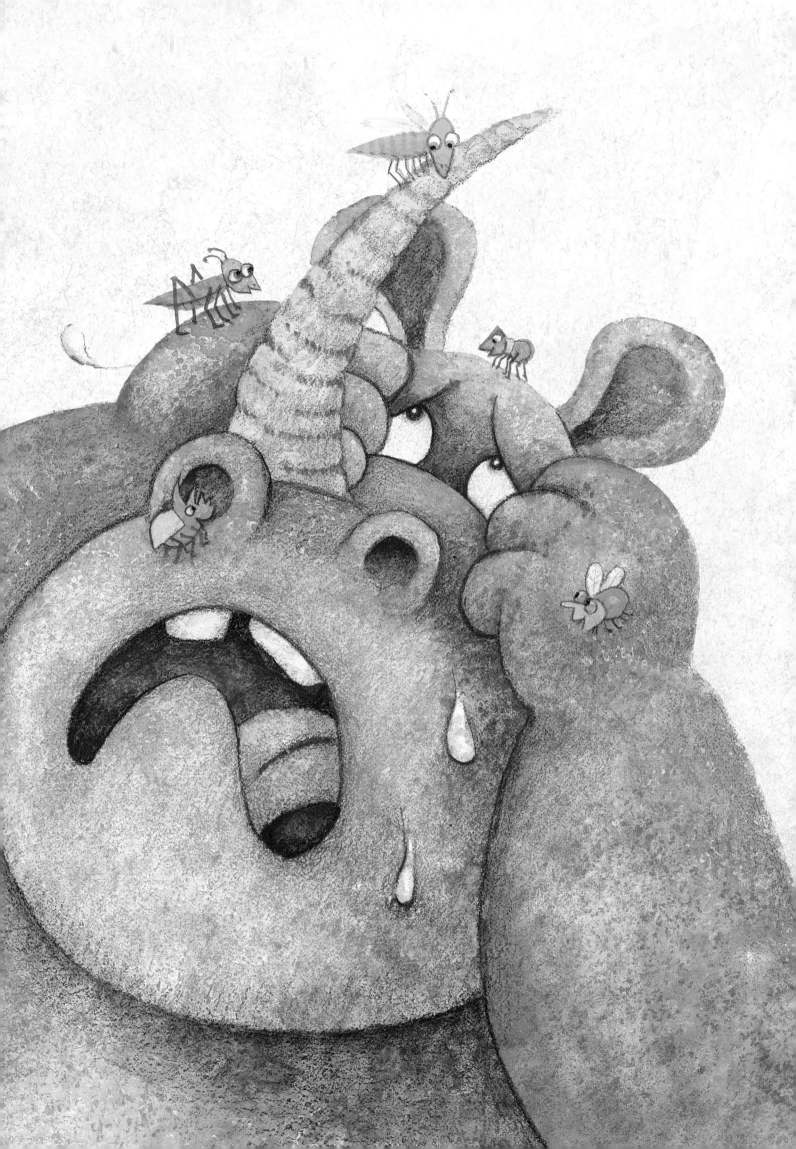

The animals rocketed onto the slide
For an up-and-down, all-around fabulous ride.

They swooped, and they bounced, and they looped, and they pounced.
Then Takoda the tiger cub proudly announced,
"Our zoo is the best because

everyone counts!"

The New Insect Zoo

What sport do bugs like best?

Cricket, of course.

What's the World's biggest ant?

An elephant.

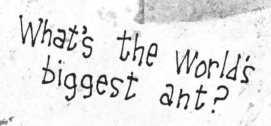

Why are beetles such poor dancers?

Because they have 3 left feet.

How many bees are in a hive?

Just count the legs and divide by 6.

What has 5 wings and 2 stingers?

A wasp with spare parts.